... illustrator in a garden shed ... Machynlleth. He drew for Michael Morpurgo and Rose Impey, but people kept encouraging him to write. Many years and more than 175 books later, Shoo has built a worldwide following for his award-winning how-to-draw videos on YouTube. http://www.shoorayner.com/

Shoo lives in the Forest of Dean with his wife and three cats.

Shoo says about *Dragon Gold*: 'I've kept chickens and a few cats in my time. I think a pet dragon would be like a mixture of the two!'

Dragon Gold

For Penny and Janet,
Thanks for letting me be a Firefly!

First published in 2014
by Firefly Press
25 Gabalfa Road, Llandaff North, Cardiff, CF14 2JJ
www.fireflypress.co.uk

A CIP catalogue record of this book is available from the British Library.

Print ISBN: 978-1-910080-04-7
Epub ISBN: 978-1-910080-05-4

This book has been published with the support of the Welsh Books Council.

Typeset by: Elaine Sharples

Printed and bound by: Bell and Bain, Glasgow

Dragon Gold

Shoo Rayner

Firefly

Chapter One

Harri

'Woah! Is that you, Harri?' Megan called across the street. 'How did you get your eyeball to fall out like that?'

Considering it was 8.30 in the morning and there were three days until Halloween, there were a lot of ghosts, mummies, zombies and witches walking down the street on their way to school.

Harri smiled happily under his zombie mask, though you would never know it from the hideous green and purple make-up that made his face look like he'd been dead for a couple of years.

Yes! thought Harri. *All my hard work has paid off. I'm going to win the Dressing-up Day competition, no question.*

Harri had been working on his costume all week. He'd made a papier-mâché mask and used long

1

strings of matted wool for hair. His eyeball, which seemed to dangle out of its socket, was made from a ping-pong ball. It was brilliant.

Mrs Ellis in the charity shop next door had helped him find some really old clothes. He'd ripped them up and covered them in blobs of red paint. Old lace-up boots, far too big for him, finished off the whole look. They made him walk in that slow, clumsy way that zombies are meant to.

'Oh Harri, you look amazing!' said his friend, Ben. All the kids gathered around him in the playground ooh-ing and aah-ing. Everyone agreed his was the best costume and Harri was definitely going to win the competition.

Then, in the distance, they heard a car engine revving up. They all knew who it was. Ryan's dad had a huge, black Range Rover Evoque – you know, one that looks like a cat that's about to pounce. It had darkened windows so you couldn't see in.

Ryan could easily walk to school in the morning. He

lived only half a mile down the road. But no, his dad had to drive him in that enormous car. Every day Mr Sayer, the crossing patrol man, would leap into the road and make him wait. While Mr Sayer helped a gaggle of infants across the road, Ryan's dad would rev the car impatiently.

Normally he'd let Ryan out, turn round in the pub car park and drive noisily back home again.

But today he turned into the school gates and parked in the middle of the playground.

'OMG!' Megan shrieked. 'Everyone knows you're not allowed to do that! If Mrs Yates sees, Ryan will be for it … and so will his dad!'

Sometimes it seemed that Mrs Yates, the Head Teacher, had nothing to do other than battle against naughty parents who didn't do what they were told.

Loudspeakers had been tied onto the car's roof rack. With a crackle and a hum, they came to life. Scary music filled the playground.

'That's *Carmina Burana*,' Jack said. 'They use that

3

music in loads of horror films.' Jack was dressed as Dracula. He was obsessed with old horror films. This was his second favourite day of the year. Halloween came first. He could win *Mastermind* with horror films as his specialist subject.

A football rolled towards the car. No one bothered to chase after it. Everyone stopped doing what they were doing and watched. Even the mums and teachers were mesmerised. They stood, glued to the ground, staring open-mouthed, as Ryan's dad slowly climbed out of the car.

He wore a black suit with a black pork pie hat, black leather gloves and wrap-around dark sunglasses.

Acting like a chauffeur, he swaggered to the back door and opened it a crack. Smoke oozed out from the edges of the door. It crept down the side of the car and swept across the playground.

The music boomed louder as the tempo increased. The voices on the music sounded like they were singing in the burning fires of hell.

Ryan's dad swung the door wide open. Lights flashed inside making the smoke change colours. It looked like the burning fires of hell were actually inside the car!

Ryan's dad had a tiny microphone headset. He was a DJ, when he could be bothered, so he had all the equipment. He pressed a switch near his ear and spoke in a deep, cheesy American accent.

'Behold!' His voice boomed across the playground from the loud speakers. **'Behold! The Angel of Death!'**

'O … M … G …!' Megan shrieked.

The Angel of Death emerged from the back seat of the Range Rover. It was easily over two metres high and its wings stretched out at least two metres on either side.

It had no face. The hood on the ragged black cloak was empty. No head!

A stream of smoke poured out of the void where its head should have been. Megan screamed.

As Ryan's dad drove off and the music faded away, the Angel of Death walked slowly over to the group of children that had been admiring Harri's costume. It walked in a ghostly, ethereal manner. The dark emptiness of its hood glared down at them.

'OMG!' Megan whispered. 'It's like something out of *Doctor Who*!'

From the depths of nowhere a strange, electronic voice spoke.

'Nice costume Harri! What do you think of mine?'

'Ryan? Is that you?'

Slowly, the cloth lifted to reveal Ryan's freckled face, looking out of a dark, see-through window sewn in the chest of his suit.

'OMG!' said Megan. 'That is the most amazing costume I've ever seen in all my life.'

'Dad helped a bit,' said Ryan, lifting up the wafty skirts of his cloak to show the high-tech stilts he had

7

strapped to his legs to make him look taller, and the can of smoke effect that blew out of the empty hood on top of his head. His wings stretched out wide on sticks that were strapped to Ryan's hands. The whole effect was amazing.

'Doesn't he look great, Harri?' Jack asked.

'Yeah, great!' Harri growled.

He's going to win again, thought Harri. *Or rather his dad is going to win again!*

Imelda Spelltravers

In a town close by, an old lady got ready for her first meeting of the day. She wore a long green velvet cloak held together at the neck with a huge diamond-covered star. Her pointed hat was a little bit crumpled.

Anyone watching her might think it looked like a witch's hat. But no one *was* watching her. She had a way of making herself almost invisible. In fact, if you noticed her, you would be surprised by the way people walked right past her as if she wasn't there.

Her meeting was at a shop called The Crystal Cave. She reached for the door handle and whispered words of courage to herself.

> 'Blow your nose,
>
> Tap your shoes.
>
> Spit on your eyebrows –
>
> Nothing to lose.'

The bell tinkled as she walked in and introduced herself.

Ryan's Dad

Ryan's dad went home and got changed into jeans and a T-shirt. He made a cup of coffee and settled down to watch daytime TV with the paper and a packet of milk chocolate digestive biscuits.

* * *

'Well, children! Don't you all look amazing?' Mrs Yates beamed from the front of the school hall. There were zombies, vampires and monsters of every description. Aliens from a multitude of planets and primping, pink princesses sat in rows before her. Princesses?

Harri was a serious dresser-up. *What did princesses have to do with Halloween?* he thought. It was always the same girls too. Whatever they were asked to dress up as, they always put on the

bridesmaid's dress they wore to their auntie's wedding and came as princesses.

No one tried as hard as he did to make a great and original costume. So many kids got their outfits ready-made from the supermarket, where they hung in rows with all the other Halloween stuff.

And then there was Ryan, brooding over them all at the back of the hall. Ryan had to lean against the gym equipment so he didn't fall over. He couldn't sit on the floor like everyone else.

'We have a special visitor with us today,' said Mrs Yates, who could hardly contain her excitement. 'Mrs Eileen Spelltravers is a famous children's author. She writes the very successful *Happy Witch* stories and she is going to read one for us today. Isn't that exciting, children?'

Mrs Yates explained how Mrs Spelltravers had written 23 *Happy Witch* stories which were famous all over the world.

11

'Now, I want you all to give Mrs Spelltravers a big, warm school welcome.'

The children cheered and clapped as the two women shook hands. Mrs Yates sat down in her chair and smiled as if she was going to burst with happiness.

'Good Morning, children!' said the very smiley Mrs Spelltravers.

'Good morning, Miss Smelltravers. Good morning ev-ree-one,' came the reply.

'This is the *Happy Witch*,' Miss Spelltravers warbled, holding up a copy of her book. The *Happy Witch* wore a long green velvet cloak held together at the neck with huge diamond-covered star. Her pointed witch's hat was a bit crumpled.

Mrs Spelltravers read the story. Harri loved stories, but he thought the *Happy Witch* didn't really do a lot. The book was really for the tiddlers in reception.

'Does anybody have any questions?' Mrs Yates asked, when the story was over.

Harri put his hand up. 'Do you do the drawings? I thought they were really good.'

Mrs Spelltravers smiled politely. 'No, I just write the stories. My wonderful daughter, Jane, is the illustrator. *She* does all the pictures.'

* * *

'Goodbye, and thank you for your time,' the old lady in the long green velvet cloak sighed as she closed the door of The Crystal Cave.

'Where next?' she asked herself, as she consulted her notebook.

Anyone who noticed her there on the street would have said that she just sort of … disappeared. But as no one did notice her, it didn't matter if she did or she didn't.

Ryan's dad turned the TV volume down, folded the newspaper over his head and shut his eyes. He'd got up earlier than usual today. Ryan's mum had an important meeting to get to and then there was Ryan's big entrance at school. That was a lot of work.

We're going to win with that costume, no problem, he thought. A look of satisfaction crept over his face as he fell asleep.

* * *

Assembly was nearly over. Just one more thing – the most important thing – the most important thing of the last few weeks. The Dressing-up Day competition.

Each year group paraded around the edge of the hall showing off their costumes, while Mr Davies'

iPod played Michael Jackson's *Thriller* over the school's music system.

Some kids did a bit of bad acting, snarling and clumping about as if they were dead. The princesses floated along with dreamy far-away looks, imagining that one day a prince would come along on a big white horse and take them away from all this school nonsense.

'I blame the Disney channel!' Harri mumbled.

'Mrs Spelltravers has graciously agreed to choose one winner from each year group and an overall winner too,' Mrs Yates announced.

It took forever to get round to Harri's year. Harri turned on the full zombie works. He staggered and moaned and groaned. He clawed the air and rolled his remaining eyeball as if he had just woken up and crawled out of the grave. As he went past Mrs Spelltravers he shook his dangling eyeball vigorously and snarled at her, so she could see all the hard work he'd put into his costume.

Mrs Spelltravers giggled and winked at Mrs Yates.

Harri could hear Ryan close behind him. His stilted feet clumped on the wooden floor. His costume hissed as smoke spilled out of the empty hood. He could feel a cool wind on his back as Ryan flapped his enormous wings.

'Oh! Ha ha! And who do we have here?' Mrs Spelltravers laughed nervously.

Ryan stopped and stood motionless. Slowly, really slowly, like he'd rehearsed it a hundred times, he turned his empty head towards Mrs Spelltravers. He held her gaze with his invisible eyes. Then, just when Mrs Spelltravers was starting to feel a little uncomfortable, he let a stream of smoke blast her way.

'Oh!' Mrs Spelltravers squeaked. 'Oh, very good. Ha ha!'

Harri knew the game was over. As Mrs Spelltravers gave out the prizes, it became obvious that she was one of those people who didn't understand dressing-up. The winners she chose from each year were mostly wearing costumes bought from the supermarket.

Anyone can do that, thought Harri. *That's not a proper costume.*

She even chose a princess!

'Such a pretty frock, my dear,' Mrs Spelltravers cooed, as she gave Chelsey Owen a signed copy of one of her books. 'You must have been the prettiest bridesmaid of the year!'

Chelsey sashayed back to her place on the hall floor and sat down like a pink, shiny, satin meringue, smiling as only a princess who's kissed a frog can smile.

And of course Ryan won his year group competition and… 'And the overall winner of this year's Dressing-up Day competition goes to … The

18

Angel of Death, Ryan Williams!' Mrs Yates announced.

Mr Davies found the Darth Vader music on his iPod and everyone cheered and sang along as Ryan swept up the side of the hall to receive his prize.

'Dum-dum-dum dum-di-dum dum-di-dum!'

Mrs Spelltravers tried to shake his wing and gave him a signed boxed set of the *Happy Witch* stories and a goody bag of *Happy Witch* stuff including a T-shirt, DVD, magic sweets and a doll wearing a green cloak held together with a diamond star and a pointy, crumpled witch's hat.

Mrs Spelltravers looked up into the empty face of the Angel of Death. 'The T-shirt might be a bit small for you, dear,' she joked. 'But the books are collector's editions. Now don't go selling them on eBay,' she giggled.

Ryan remained silent and mysterious. He bowed graciously with his enormous wings, accepted his

prize and blew smoke right into Mrs Spelltravers' face. She spluttered and nearly fell over backwards.

'Thank you Ryan, and well done!' Mrs Yates smiled through gritted teeth.

Mrs Spelltravers had now succumbed to a loud coughing fit. Mrs Yates took a firm grip of her arm and guided her out of the hall.

'Come along, Eileen. I think you deserve a nice cup of coffee in the staff room,' she said.

Harri could hardly believe it. It was so obvious Ryan hadn't made his own costume. Any fool could tell it was his dad who'd made it.

It wasn't about the prize. It was never about the prize. It was about winning fair and square. Anyway, who wanted to win a stupid *Happy Witch* doll and books?

Life was so unfair. Ryan won every competition going, or rather his dad did. That's all Ryan's dad cared about. Making sure that Ryan won all the school competitions and that he got top marks for his homework. Ryan's dad was really good at homework!

Ryan's dad slept peacefully. There would be no homework over half-term. He could relax for a bit before he packed up the Range Rover. They were off to the airport tonight for a week's holiday in their cottage in France. Lovely!

* * *

Mr. Davies

'Well done Ryan!' Mr Davies boomed, as he walked into class. There'd been an early break after assembly. Everyone's costumes looked a little tired from running around the playground. Ryan's costume was so cumbersome, he'd taken it off.

The cloak, hood and wings hung over the book cupboard door. The stilts leaned against the wall, looking like legs that had fallen off a robot.

'Your dad did a wonderful job with your Angel of Death costume,' Mr Davies said with a sarcastic tone in his voice. Harri rejoiced for a moment. Mr Davies understood. He knew that the winner of a dressing-up competition should be the person who made the best costume *by themselves.*

Then he spoiled it. 'How did you do the smoke effect?' he asked earnestly. 'That was amazing!'

Mr Davies was truly interested as Ryan showed him the can of smoke and how it was connected to a tube at the back of the hood.

'And this is the electronic voice-changing unit that makes my voice sound like a Dalek,' Ryan explained.

Mr Davies secretly admired Ryan's dad and the ingenious skill he showed when 'helping' Ryan with his homework projects.

There was nothing Harri could do. But he was determined to get even somehow – one day.

Chapter Two

The rivalry had been going on since reception year, when Harri and Ryan were first put together in the same class.

You name it, Ryan's dad had won or done everything.

In infants, Ryan had been Joseph in the school nativity play. Ryan's dad had got a real donkey. When Ryan led Mary down the hall to the stable at the inn, the donkey lifted its tail and pooed all over the Mayor's shoes. The audience loved it! Ryan bowed and took his applause. His dad videoed the whole thing, they got £250 when they sent it to *You've Been Framed* and it was shown on TV. You can see it on YouTube. It's had millions of views.

Ryan's dad was Ryan's personal football, tennis, swimming and running coach. He helped out with sport's day and somehow Ryan always managed to

win everything. Ryan was the school football captain too, even though he wasn't the best player.

Ryan's dad did the school discos, so Ryan always won the best dancer competition.

Ryan's dad made the scenery and effects for the school plays. Maybe Ryan didn't get the lead role, but he always got the best part. He was an alien once, with moving tentacles and flashing lights. He totally stole the show.

He was just one of the gangster's mob in *Bugsy Malone*, but his dad made him a gun that fired marshmallows into the audience. That was a real hit.

Whatever Ryan did, his dad made sure he did it better than anyone else.

However sorry for himself Harri felt, he was beyond getting cross about it. There was just no point. The most annoying thing about Ryan was that he was a really nice guy. Not a best friend, but a friend. And his dad was good fun too. He was full of jokes, always had good ideas and was really

generous. Ryan's birthday parties were the best and everyone got invited.

Harri stared out the window. A crocodile of nursery kids toddled on a nature walk along the playing field hedge. *It would be so nice to win something … just once,* he thought.

'Well, I don't suppose we'll get much work done this morning,' Mr Davies sighed. 'You kids are wound up like clockwork springs. We should send you home early, you're not going to learn anything today.'

The whole class cheered and began packing up their things.

'No!' Mr Davies groaned. 'I didn't say you *could* go home, I said you *should* go home. Everyone sit down and face the front.

'Now, what did you think of the *Happy Witch* story that Mrs Spelltravers told this morning?' Mr Davies asked when everyone had settled down.

'Boring!' the class groaned in unison.

'Oh sir,' Jack complained, 'it was for babies!'

25

'I liked the pictures,' said Harri.

Mr Davies smiled. Harri was a bit of a dreamer. That's what made him the best artist in the class. Harri loved drawing and making stuff.

'That's a really good zombie costume, Harri,' said Mr Davies. 'Did you make it yourself?'

Harri beamed with delight and waggled his dangling eye. At last someone had officially noticed his costume. For a minute he explained how he'd made it and how hard it had been getting all the things he needed and how difficult it had been pushing each woollen hair into the papier-mâché head.

'Well done,' said Mr Davies. 'You have a real flair for art, don't you, Harri?' Then he turned to Ryan and asked if they could look at one of the books he'd won.

Mr Davies held up the book so they could all see. 'Did anyone notice anything about the pictures?' he asked.

Harri's hand shot up. Everyone else shook their heads and looked blank. Mr Davies smiled.

'Well, Harri?'

'Sir, it was the dragons.'

'Yes!' Mr Davies punched the air. 'Can you tell us what it was about the dragons, Harri?'

'Well, the dragons weren't mentioned in the story, but they were there in all the pictures, fighting each other in the background. It was like they had a story of their own going on. The red dragon won!'

'Well done, Harri,' Mr Davies beamed. 'And can anyone tell me why those dragons were in the story?'

Harri wasn't quite sure, but he had an idea. Slowly, hesitating, he raised his finger. 'Are they Welsh Dragons?'

'Yes!' cheered Mr Davies. 'They are Welsh dragons, indeed.' Mr Davies held up the picture. The whole class strained to see the tiny dragons that were drawn in the background of the pictures.

'One of the dragons is Welsh,' Mr Davies explained. 'The illustrator has added a whole other story in the pictures. It comes from the *Mabinogion*.'

28

The whole class groaned. Mr Davies was obsessed with the *Mabinogion* and all the other tales of ancient Wales. They got him really excited. He could go on about the olden days for hours. In fact, over half-term, Mr Davies was going to an Ancient Welsh versus Saxon Invaders re-enactment battle.

Mr and Mrs Davies, and their two little children, were going to dress up as ancient Welsh warriors, sleep in a wet field, in a leaking tent, and eat authentic, rotten medieval food, so that they could have a mock battle with a load of people dressed up as ancient Saxons.

Last year, Mr Davies had come back to school with a broken arm. He told everyone he'd been defending the nation from the Saxon marauders. The truth came out in the end. He'd drunk a bit too much mead. In the middle of the night, he'd fallen over a tent rope on his way to the toilet and ended up in the Emergency Department. He'd completely missed the battle.

'Let me tell you about the plague that tormented the Island of Briton in the reign of King Lludd,' Mr Davies said mysteriously.

Everyone in the class rolled their eyes. Mr Davies was going off on one of his stories. But no one really minded. Mr Davies was a brilliant storyteller. He could do voices and sound effects and a very good impression of Mrs Yates, the Head Teacher.

* * *

'Every year, on the eve of May Day, when all should be rejoicing at the coming of summer, the air would be split asunder by a shrieking cry, louder than thunder or the crash of lightning. The eerie screams echoed across the entire land, shaking the mountains to their very foundations. Such was the pain in those cries that they tore at the hearts

of all who heard them, draining the blood of men, leaving them pale as wraiths. Women lost their unborn children and cried tears that filled rivers and streams. Young men and girls lost their senses, running through the streets in wild, hysterical confusion. The worlds of animals and trees and all that lived in the air or under the waters were devastated. Animals cowered in their nests and lairs and the trees were shaken to their very roots.'

Mr Davies had got the attention of the whole class now. They sat at their desks, open-mouthed, goggle-eyed, as he spun his story.

'The minds of all who lived in Britain were enfeebled. No one knew the cause of the terrible plague. The people's spirits were so disaffected, their will so weakened, they had no idea how to rid themselves of this annual horror.

31

'Llefelys, the King of the Gauls, was King Lludd's brother. He knew the cause and counselled his brother with good advice. "Dragons!" Llefelys whispered, lest anyone else should hear.

'"Set a trap in the very centre of the country," he said. "At the height of the battle the dragons will turn into pigs, for that is how they disguise themselves for the rest of the year. When they fall to the ground, capture them and send them to sleep in a butt of strong mead."'

'Isn't that how you broke your arm last year, sir?' Jack asked. The class broke into a snuffle of stifled giggles.

'Thank you, Jack!' Mr Davies said, wearily. He'd never been allowed to forget about his Ancient Welsh midnight manoeuvres! But he was in full swing now and nothing was going to put him off his story. He continued.

'Llefelys advised his brother to imprison the dragons in a stone coffer and bury them far underground, so they could never come back to haunt the land again.

'King Lludd measured the whole land of Britain and determined that the centre of the country was at Oxford. He ordered a huge pit to be dug and in the middle a giant, wooden butt was constructed.'

Mr Davies sighed deeply. 'Why are you sniggering, Connor?'

Connor could hardly get the words out for laughing. 'You said *butt*, sir!'

Mr Davies rolled his eye to the heavens. 'A butt is a container for liquids, Connor. They would have made it from wooden planks, like a giant beer barrel.'

'Not a *mead* barrel then, sir?' Jack giggled.

Mr Davies pretended he hadn't heard. He took a deep breath and carried on with the story.

'On the eve of May Day, King Lludd ordered the butt to be filled with strong mead, then the pit was covered in silk to hide the trap beneath. King Lludd and his men filled their ears with wax, wrapped their heads with heavy woollen scarves and waited.

'As the sun sank slowly in the west and the moon rose to join the twinkling stars, the onslaught of sound and fury began. Two dragons, one white and one red, fought each other in the skies above the country.

34

'Relentless they were and deafening was the sound as their talons slashed the horny armour of their scales. The screams of pain and fury, as they clashed and smashed each other, rang out across the nation. Even with their ears blocked, King Lludd and his men were shaken and frozen with fear.

'As the night drew on, the battle grew in intensity and ferocity until, high above in the skies of Oxfordshire, the exhausted creatures

gave up their fight. Just as King Llefelys had said, the dragons slowly turned into pigs as they fell through the darkening sky. Down they fell. Down and down. The silk enveloped them as they crashed into the giant butt of mead.

'Thirsty from their battling, the dragon pigs drank deeply and were soon overcome by a deep sleep.

'In awe, and still shaken from the screams, King Lludd and his men sprang into action. They tied the sleeping dragon-pigs up in the silk cloth and incarcerated them in a stone coffer that had been made specially for the occasion. With a team of twelve oxen, the coffer was hauled all the way to Dinas Emrys, the strongest fortress in the land. There the coffer was buried for all time, deep beneath the ground.

'The next May Day saw great rejoicing, for the dragons had been silenced and men, women and children could dance freely round the maypoles

and welcome the coming of summer and the arrival of peace upon the land. Soon the dragons were forgotten, consigned to history and distant memory, though they were not dead, but only sleeping...'

Ben broke the silence. 'Is that true, sir?'

'Maybe...' Mr Davies said mysteriously. 'Dinas Emrys is real. Look, here it is in the illustrations in the book. It's not all that far from here.' Mr Davies raised a quizzical eyebrow. 'So, maybe the story *is* true?'

The bell rang for the end of class and the spell was broken by the banging of desks and the scraping of chairs.

'We'll do more about dragons this afternoon,' Mr Davies shouted into the din. No one in the class was listening. All they could think about was their empty stomachs.

* * *

'Goodbye, and thank you for your time,' the old lady in the long green velvet cloak sighed as she closed the door of Moonspell's Alternative Gifts and Remedies.

'Time for some lunch,' she told herself.

Anyone who noticed her there on the bench in the High Street, eating a sandwich and pouring a cup of tea from a flask might have thought it was a strange time of year for a picnic. But no one did notice her. It was almost as though she was invisible.

'Now where next?' she asked herself, consulting her notebook again.

* * *

Ryan's Dad popped a meal into the microwave and began ticking things off the list his wife had left him.

Passports

Suitcases

Money

Travel documents and tickets

Coats and backpacks

Everything was ready. Mrs W. would be home from work early, they'd pick Ryan up from school and get straight on their way to the airport. It was lucky that Ryan's Angel of Death costume hadn't needed any face painting. 'What would they say about that in airport security?' he laughed as he tucked into his *Weight Watchers* chicken and mango curry.

* * *

 'Look, sir,' Harri said in class that afternoon. 'I found a book about dragons in the library. I've borrowed it for half-term.'

Harri should have known a lot about dragons.

Merlin's Cave, the shop where he lived, was full of them. There were model dragons of all shapes and sizes. Most of them would fit in the palm of your hand. Some were very detailed, others were a bit cartoony and jokey. One was amazing. It was about forty centimetres high. It was a serpent really, its scaly body coiled around a crystal ball. It looked so real you would think it was alive.

It was £129.99 so they kept it on the top shelf behind the counter, out of harm's way. It looked awesome, but no one had bought it yet.

The class spent the afternoon drawing and writing about dragons.

'Can dragons really fly, sir?' Connor asked.

'That depends on whether you believe in dragons or not,' Mr Davies laughed.

'No, I mean really,' said Connor. 'I mean are there real dragons and can they fly?'

'Well, there are Komodo dragons,' said Mr Davies. 'They'll eat you up if they catch you, and

they can run really fast when they want to. And there are bearded dragons which people have as pets.'

'Oh, look!' Harri pointed at a page in his book. 'There are. Look here. There are real flying dragon lizards!'

Everyone crowded round to have a look.

'But they're just lizards with wings,' Jack grumbled. 'They don't breathe fire or anything exciting, do they?'

'Wouldn't it be great if you could make a model dragon that could fly and really breathe fire and stuff like that?' Harri mused.

'Duh!' Megan flicked Harri's dangling eyeball. Harri was determined to wear his zombie costume all day. 'How would you do that then?'

Harri shrugged. 'I don't know, electric motors and fireworks, I suppose.'

Mr Davies' eyes twinkled. He'd had an idea. 'Right,' he said, getting everyone's attention. 'Here's

41

a challenge! There will be a bag of Dragon Gold for anyone who can make a dragon fly for more than ten seconds at the school Eisteddfod on St David's Day, the first of March next year.'

As well as singing, reciting poetry and playing music, they always had a making competition at the school Eisteddfod. Every year, Mr Davies had trouble thinking up something new and exciting to set as the theme of the making project. This was perfect. Dragons were a good Welsh theme for St David's Day and it might make the children learn some more ancient Welsh history too.

While the other kids asked him all sorts of questions about what they were allowed to make the model with and how big it should be and did it really have to fly, Harri caught Ryan's eye from across the classroom. It was a fleeting moment, but they both knew the game was on. This was going to be a serious competition.

Chapter Three

Mr. Davies

'Here are the rules,' said Mr Davies. As he typed them on his laptop, the projector spilled the words across the white board.

There will be a bag of Dragon Gold for anyone who can make a dragon fly for more than ten seconds at the school Eisteddfod on St David's Day, the first of March next year.

'I'll put it on the class web page now,' he said. 'You can interpret the rules as you wish.'

The bell rang for the end of the day. The school erupted like a volcano pouring its molten lava of screaming children into the playground. It was half-term. No more school for over a week!

'Ah, there it is,' said the old lady in the long green velvet cloak. 'Merlin's Cave.' She looked up at the sky and judged the time of day. The sun was low over the hills that cradled the little town of St Gertrude's. The leaves fell from the trees and ran about the streets in the crisp wind, skittering around her feet like kittens chasing one another.

The thought of feet made her feel like having a bit of a sit down and a nice cup of tea. 'I'll pop back later. It'll be my last visit of the day,' she told herself.

The library across the road had a little café. That would do nicely. She bought herself a cup of tea and sat quietly in a corner, reading a book about herbal remedies that she found in the dark, dusty folklore section of the library.

Anyone noticing her there might wonder why she chuckled every time she found a mistake in the book. No one did notice. You could almost say she was invisible.

 Ryan's dad greeted Harri as he crossed the street after school. 'Wow, Harri! That is a great costume, did you make it yourself? You are *so* creative.'

See? It was impossible not to like Ryan's dad. He was just so nice!

Harri took being a zombie seriously. Most of the other kids had discarded parts of their costumes during the day, or their make-up had smeared and now they looked like bruised fruit.

'See ya, Harri! Hi, Mr Williams!' Jack ran past them and waved. His greased-back Dracula hair now stood up on end. The lipstick bloodstains on his face had smeared down his chin and were all over the collar of his best white shirt. His mum would be furious when she saw it.

'Neat,' Ryan's dad said, as he inspected Harri's costume. 'Did you poke all the hair in by hand? That's amazing. And that eyeball is so realistic, well done!'

See? Not only was he a nice guy, but he was the only one who really understood how much work Harri had put into his costume. They were fellow artists!

Ryan arrived carrying the parts of his costume. His dad raised his eyebrows, hope and expectation all over his face. 'Well...?'

Ryan dropped his shoulders and looked sad for a moment, disappointed even. Then his face cracked into a smile. He held up his bag full of *Happy Witch* stuff and cheered. 'First prize!'

Ryan's dad punched the air. It was amazing how happy the news made him. He looked in the bag to see what they had won. 'Oh, this stuff is for babies.' He sounded disappointed. 'Never mind.' He smiled. 'We can always sell it on eBay.'

'That's what the lady said!' Ryan laughed as he tossed his stuff in the boot of the car. 'See ya next week, Harri!' He jumped in the back of the car and slammed the heavy door shut.

Ryan's mum rolled her eyes at Harri. 'What are they like, eh?'

The car revved up and they were gone. It was half-term.

* * *

 The old-fashioned brass bell tinkled as Harri opened the door of the shop. Dylan the cat stretched himself in the window and settled back down in the last rays of sunshine.

'Is that you, Harri?' his mum called out from the stockroom at the back of the shop.

'Yeah!' he sighed deeply.

'Oh, pet.' Harri's mum poked her head around the corner and peered over the rack of incense and herbal candles. 'Didn't you win, then?'

'No.' Harri sighed again.

'What was it this time?' Ryan and his dad had been winning everything for so long, she didn't need to ask who'd won the dressing-up competition.

Harri told her about his day. 'Ryan's costume *was* amazing, though,' he admitted.

'That's not the point,' his mum said. 'Ryan's dad does everything for that child. He lives his life through him. Ryan will have to stand on his own two feet one day.'

She bustled about collecting up receipts and paperwork. 'I've got to go to the bank before it closes,' she said. 'Can you get a quick snack and a glass of milk and mind the shop for a few minutes

while I'm out? Friday afternoon's always a bit slow. I don't expect we'll get any customers now.'

Harri cut a thick slice of fresh bread and smothered it with Nutella. He poured himself a glass of milk and settled down behind the counter in the shop. Dylan dropped down from the window and eased himself onto Harri's lap, seeking a bit of attention.

'I shouldn't be long. See you in a minute.' The bell tinkled as his mum slammed the door and hurried down the street.

Harri was used to working in the shop. He'd been doing little jobs for his mum for as long as he could remember – packing mail orders, stocking the shelves, sweeping up and keeping the place clean and tidy. These days he did all the computer stuff for her. She hadn't got a clue. The business would fall to bits if he didn't keep the website going for her.

He looked around the shop. It was all he'd ever known. He and his mum lived upstairs. His dad had

left when he was only two weeks old – gone off travelling around the world. He'd gone to *'find himself'*, his mum would mutter through gritted teeth. Then she'd joke, 'He couldn't find himself in a mirror! He was a loser through and through.'

Harri had a picture of his dad, smiling in front of an Inca temple in Peru. He'd sent it to Harri on his fifth birthday. Not even his grandparents had heard from him since.

Harri hoped he was like his mum, hard-working, resilient and practical. But when she talked about his dad like that, he worried that some of his dad's useless blood was in him. Was Harri going to grow up and be a loser too? He was never going to be a winner while Ryan and his dad were around, that was for sure.

Harri took one of the models of the red Welsh dragons off the shelf and started sketching it. It was one of their bestselling items. Harri knew all the shop's sales statistics. He had to keep his mum's

accounts and spreadsheets up to date on the computer. She had no idea about modern technology. Her phone still had a small grey screen and played that antique *diddy-dum-dum-dum* ringtone!

Tourists came to St Gertrude's because of the Holy Well. They bought the little red dragons as souvenirs of their visit. Apparently, St Gertrude had tripped and bashed her head against a rock. Water had sprung out of the rock, mending her broken

head instantly and, if you believed all the stories, it cured her of everything else too, from smallpox to housemaid's knee!

The story was different every time it was told, but it brought the tourists to the town. They drank the water that still poured from a lion's head that had been fixed onto St Gertrude's Rock. The water had been tested. It was incredibly pure and sweet. It was warm too, so it steamed in the winter months.

A small fridge display unit by the door of the shop was full of cold plastic bottles of St Gertrude's Water. It was another bestseller. They even sent bottles of it worldwide to people who hoped it would cure them of strange diseases.

Harri was lost in his drawing. It was always like that when he drew. That's why he loved drawing so much. Once he'd started, it was like he'd fallen into another world, a world he created as he went along. If he wanted a castle over there, he would draw it. If he wanted a cool new iPhone, he would draw it too.

Wouldn't it be amazing if the things he drew actually came to life? He often thought that. Lost in a world of drawing, you could imagine anything you liked.

Now he was drawing a dragon – a red Welsh dragon – just like the one Mr Davies had told them about this morning in school. Just like the one he'd been trying to draw all afternoon. It was much easier to get the details right with the model in front of him. Mr Davies' Eisteddfod challenge rang in his head.

He checked the school website. There it was on his class page.

Next Year's Eisteddfod Challenge:
There will be a bag of Dragon Gold for anyone who can make a dragon fly for more than ten seconds at the school Eisteddfod on St David's Day, the first of March next year.

Harri turned the dragon model and started drawing it from a different angle. How could he make a dragon fly? What would he need? Helium balloons? Hot air? Electric motors and propellers? As he drew and sketched the ideas that came to him, he began to resolve that this time – and he really meant it – he was going to win that bag of Dragon Gold!

He knew the Dragon Gold was probably only going to be one of those bags of chocolate money (a Christmas bestseller in the shop) but this time … this time he was going to beat Ryan and his dad. This time was going to be different!

Chapter Four

'Hello, my dear! That's a lovely drawing. Are you looking after the shop?'

Harri nearly fell off the chair. He hadn't heard anyone come in. An old lady in a long green velvet cloak was leaning over the counter, inspecting his drawing. In her crumpled, pointy hat, she looked just like… No! That was a ridiculous idea. The *Happy Witch* was a book for little children. This was a real person.

'Er … er … I'm sorry,' Harri stammered. 'I didn't hear you come in.'

Harri's mother was big on customer service. 'Always greet the customers with a smile when they come through the door of the shop.' She'd said it a million times, so now Harri always beamed at the customers without thinking. But now he felt a bit awkward, like he'd been caught out doing something naughty.

'Those are very good drawings,' the old lady said. Her eyes twinkled and her face crinkled into a wide smile. Harri knew she really meant it.

Dylan dropped down on the floor and curled his tail around the old lady's legs. 'Hello, puss!' Dylan purred so loudly it sounded like someone was digging up the road outside. She reached over and handed Harri a business card.

The card was printed in glossy ink that stood up from the thick card. Harri felt the expensive raised lettering with his fingertips. The card announced:

Imelda Spelltravers
Spells, Potions & Herbal Remedies
– Magic Consultant –

'Spelltravers?' Harri questioned as he read the words on the card. 'You're not…?'

'The *Happy Witch*?' The old lady raised her eyebrows. 'That's my niece, Eileen,' she sighed. 'She used me as the inspiration for all her books. She never asked me if I minded. I don't suppose I do, really.'

'She came to our school today,' Harri said.

'My niece, Eileen, was here today? Well, what a coincidence! She's so busy and important these days, I never know where she'll turn up next!' The old lady laughed.

'I really liked the pictures in the books she showed us. They looked ... well ... they look just like you,' Harri explained. 'That's why I'm drawing dragons. They were in the pictures too.'

'That's my great-niece, Jane,' the old lady said. 'Yes, she's a very talented artist and yes, I must admit, the *Happy Witch* does look like me.'

Harri told her all about the Eisteddfod challenge, and how he was thinking up ideas for making a dragon fly, when he remembered his customer service training. 'Can I help you in some way?'

'I was hoping I could help you,' said the old lady, opening her bag and displaying her wares. 'I wondered if you might like to sell some of my potions and spells in your shop.

'You're my last call of the day,' she explained. 'No one comes to me for good old-fashioned magic these days, so I've started trying to sell my spells and potions in shops, but no one seems very interested in stocking my things at all.'

Harri picked up a crumbly, green sausage. 'What's this?'

'A love potion candle,' the old lady giggled.

'It doesn't look very romantic!' Harri said. 'Maybe it's the packaging? If they were pink, or in a nice box with hearts all over it? People seem to like that kind of stuff.' He showed her their bestselling love potion. The box was covered in shiny, gold, swirly patterns. Through the clear plastic front you could see rose petals and bits of dried strawberry. 'We sell quite a few of these.'

59

The old lady read the ingredients on the back. 'This isn't a love potion. This is potpourri! All this will do is make your room smell nice for a while.'

'People buy it,' Harri sighed. 'What's that?' He picked up what looked like a chicken egg.

'*That* … is a magic egg!' the old lady said proudly.

'It doesn't look like one.' Harri examined it closely. 'Shouldn't a magic egg be covered in gold or stars?'

'That's the trouble these days.' The old lady furrowed her eyebrows. 'All anyone cares about is how things look. They don't care if things work or not. Here, give me that and let me show you.'

She took the egg and began to unscrew it. Harri's jaw dropped. It was a perfect egg. How was she unscrewing it?

'Do you really want a flying dragon?' she asked.

The question took Harri off guard. 'Well … er … yes. That would be amazing!'

She took Harri's drawing and scrunched it up. Then she rolled it around in her fingertips until it was a perfect ball, which she placed in the bottom half of the egg.

'Are you sure you want a flying dragon?' she asked. 'They can be quite a handful, you know.'

Was she crazy? Was she for real? Who knows? But there was something about her that Harri liked and trusted.

'Yes!' he whispered.

The old lady gently placed the two halves of the egg together. Harri watched in amazement as the egg twisted and screwed itself back together. The egg made an almost inaudible sigh and, for a moment, it seemed to glow. Harri thought he saw the shadow of a tiny dragon projected on the surface of the egg from the inside.

'Take great care of this.' The old lady winked at Harri. 'Put it somewhere warm and safe. It'll probably take about a week.'

Harri held the egg in his hand. Now it had weight and felt solid, like an egg. It was warm and you couldn't see a join anywhere. How could that be? You can't just unscrew an egg and screw it back again!

'Thanks!' said Harri. He wanted to help her somehow. 'Look, I don't know when my mum will get back. How about if you leave some of your things as samples and we can see if anyone wants to buy them?'

'Really?' The old lady grinned. 'That would be wonderful. I'll come back in a few weeks and see how you are getting on. Oh! And you take care of that dragon, mind.'

* * *

Anyone watching in the street would have said that the old lady in the long green velvet cloak did a little dance down the street when she came out of Merlin's Cave. But no one was watching and no one saw her. Not even Harri's mum, rushing back from the bank where the manager had seen her and asked her in for a quick chat about her overdraft.

She was far too busy wondering how the shop could make more money to notice the old lady, who was almost invisible anyway.

'Oh no! The flight's been delayed an hour,' Ryan's dad grumbled, as they checked the departure screens at the airport.

'More time for shopping in the Duty Free!' Ryan's mum smiled, as she disappeared in the direction of the perfume counter.

Ryan's dad shrugged his shoulders and looked forlornly at his son. Then his face brightened. 'So what were you saying about the school Eisteddfod?'

'We have to make a dragon fly,' said Ryan.

'A dragonfly? What's that all about?'

'No! A dragon that flies,' Ryan laughed. 'I don't know … Mr Davies put it on the class website page.'

Ryan's dad pulled an iPad out of his backpack. In moments he had the page up on the screen and was reading aloud.

'There will be a bag of Dragon Gold for anyone who can make a dragon fly for

more than ten seconds at the school Eisteddfod on St David's Day, the first of March next year.'

He thought for a second. 'Dragon Gold. I wonder what that is? Do you think it's real gold? Do you think it's worth something?'

But his mind was already turning over. He'd got the bug. It was a competition and he was determined to win it … or rather, he was determined that Ryan would win it.

'Anyone who can make a dragon fly for more than ten seconds…' he mused. 'It doesn't say what kind of dragon, does it? It can be any kind of dragon. What do you think, Ryan?'

'Yeah, I suppose so.' Ryan was distracted by an enormous display of M&Ms in the Duty Free. Ryan was easily distracted by chocolate. He sauntered over to see if he could persuade his mum to add some to her shopping basket.

65

Ryan's dad typed 'Flying Dragon' into his iPad and waited to see what the search engine came up with.

'Wow! That is so cool.' He whistled through his teeth. On the screen, among drawings of dragons and photos of lizards, was a picture of the Chinese J-20 Mighty Dragon Stealth Fighter Aircraft.

It's a dragon and it flies! He smiled to himself.

Ryan's mum returned with two, bulging shopping bags. 'You look like the cat that got the cream.'

'Ryan's going to win the school Eisteddfod challenge on St David's Day,' he said triumphantly. 'I've got it all sorted.'

Ryan's mum gave her son a long-suffering look. 'Here,' she said, 'have an M&M.'

* * *

 'What is this?!' Harri's mum held one of the old lady's green sausage-shaped love-potion candles. Her nose wrinkled in disgust.

Harry told her how he'd said they'd try and sell the old lady's stuff.

'It looks like a rancid frankfurter,' she sneered. 'No one will ever buy that. And…' She sniffed the candle. 'Eew! It stinks! Put it out the back. We don't sell rubbish like that. Whoever she is, she can take it away when she comes back. If it was up to me I'd put it straight in the bin.'

Harri put the box on the worktop in the back of the shop. He picked up the egg and turned it around in his fingers. His mum hadn't met the old lady. Harri liked her and trusted her. He ran up the stairs and quietly opened the airing cupboard next to his bedroom.

'Put it somewhere warm, she said,' Harri whispered, as he made a nest from a hand towel. He put the egg in the nest and hid them both behind the hot water cylinder.

'You'll be warm and safe here,' Harri said, then he thought he saw the egg glow again, like it did when

the old lady sealed it up. It couldn't be a real dragon's egg. Could it?

* * *

 'It's going to be *fantastique!*' Ryan's dad always spoke with a terrible french accent when they were on holiday. He'd learned quite a bit of French since they'd bought their cottage in France. Their neighbours loved their crazy '*Gallois*' from next door and encouraged his efforts to learn the language.

'*C'est formidable!*' he enthused, as he showed Ryan his plans. He'd bought pencils and a big drawing pad at the *hypermarché* and had spent most of half-term working out how he and Ryan were going to build their J-20 Mighty Dragon.

He explained how they'd have to make it out of balsa wood to keep the whole thing as light as

possible, and build powerful fan motors in the body of the aircraft. 'I reckon with a bit of fuse wire and a remote control switch we could even turn those miniature firework rockets you can get into heat-seeking missiles.'

'Wuh-muh-nuh,' Ryan nodded and munched the last of his duty free M&Ms. He'd rather be taking out assassins or mining for stuff on his game console.

His dad glowed with satisfaction as he studied the plans. 'It's going to be *incroyable*! I can't wait to get started.'

* * *

The Red and White Dragon flags fluttered in the breeze. Two armies faced each other in a dank, misty valley.

'Cha-a-a-a-rge!' Mr Davies stabbed the air with his sword. Forty hairy, bearded, valiant Welshmen

followed him and threw themselves into battle against the evil, invading Saxon army. Mr Davies was having a wonderful half-term!

The trouble with running a shop is that you never get a break. Half-term and the holidays are the busiest times, especially in a tourist town like St Gertrude's.

'"What shall we do this half-term?" a million families ask themselves.' Harri was feeling a little sarcastic. '"Oh!" they say. "Let's have a great day out, tasting the water and staring into the Holy Well in St Gertrude's! We can eat St Gertrude's Pies for lunch and buy a little red dragon for a souvenir before we go home again!"'

'Don't knock the tourists.' Harri's mum scowled. 'They pay the bills. I just wish we could sell a bit more and make a little more profit to keep the bank manager happy.'

Harri had spent most of the week helping around the shop or playing video games. He'd also been looking stuff up on the internet and had even gone over the road to the library, in search of more

information about dragons. The trouble with dragons was that people just made stuff up. Since dragons didn't really exist, they wrote whatever they liked about them. Most of it was complete fantasy. There were hundreds of websites about dragons. Some people had very definite ideas about them and got quite angry if anyone contradicted them.

The library had a couple of books and, with the book he'd borrowed from school as well, Harri spent several hours snuggled up on the sofa with Dylan, learning everything he could about the history of dragons.

'Are we doing anything on Sunday?' Harri asked.

'You know Sundays are the busiest day,' Mum sighed. 'Especially at half-term.'

'How about Monday?' Harri looked bored and dejected. His mother felt quite sorry for him.

'Aren't you back to school on Monday?'

'No, don't you remember? It's a training day for the teachers. We have an extra day off.'

'Oh, Mondays after half-term are always a waste of time,' said Mum. 'Okay, let's have a day away from the shop. What would you like to do?'

'Can we go to Dinas Emrys?' Harri pleaded. 'Merlin lived there. It's where the Welsh Dragon comes from too. It's not far away.'

* * *

'Is that it?' said Harri's mum. 'I thought there'd be gift shops and a visitor centre. This is like the middle of nowhere!'

She parked the van in a lay-by at the base of Dinas Emrys. You wouldn't call it a mountain or anything. In the middle of Snowdonia, surrounded by real mountains, it was just a little bump in the landscape.

'Can we have our sandwiches up there?' Harri asked.

His mum pulled a face. 'It's a bit of a hike.'

73

'Oh Mum! We've done nothing over half-term. Ple-e-e-ease?'

It was a hard climb to the top, mostly because there wasn't really a footpath.

'You'd think there'd be signposts all over the place if it's meant to be so famous,' Harri's mum complained.

The website they'd found said to ask the National Trust for permission to climb up. Harri's mum had phoned the number and explained that Harri was doing a project at school and wanted to take photographs.

After a steep climb, a sheep track led them out onto the craggy summit. It was a perfect place for a fortress. Invaders could only attack from the bottom of the valley. You'd see them coming for miles.

Everywhere the trees were turning bare and leaves covered the ground. The waters of Llyn Dinas sparkled below them in the late autumn sun.

'And you say that Merlin lived here?' Harri's mum poured tea from a Thermos flask.

'Mum! You don't know anything,' Harri scolded. 'You run a shop called Merlin's Cave and you know nothing about him!'

'The shop was already called that when I took it over,' she replied. 'I mean, I know he was a magician and there was King Arthur and the Knights of the Round Table, but I thought that was all fairy tales.'

'No, he was real, and he was here.' Harri began telling his mother the rest of the story of the Red Dragon of Wales. He'd learned all about it over half-term from the books he'd borrowed.

'It's real history, nothing to do with King Arthur. That's fairy stories,' he explained. 'King Vortigern built a fortress right here at Dinas Emrys, except that every night while they were building it, the hillside shook and in the morning all the walls had fallen down. Well, King Vortigern didn't know what to do, so he called up his council of wise men and Druids.

'The Druids had a vision and told him to seek out

75

a fatherless boy and sacrifice him and sprinkle his blood all over the hill.'

'Eew!' his mother complained. 'I'm eating my sandwiches!'

Harri ignored her. 'Messengers were sent out to find such a boy and they eventually returned with Merlin, except he was called Emrys in those days.'

'"Wait a minute!" Emrys cried, as they were just about to cut his throat. "Killing me isn't going to solve anything." He led them to a place where he ordered them to dig, and told them that they would find a cave with a pool of water underneath.

'Well, Emrys, or Merlin, knew what he was talking about, because he'd been born a wizard. And, sure enough, when they dug down, they found the cave and there, in the pool of water, they found a stone coffer.'

'You really know about this stuff, don't you?' his mother smiled.

'Yup!' Harri went on with the story. 'And in the

76

stone coffer, wrapped in silk, were the red and white dragons that King Lludd had captured and imprisoned there. They had been disturbed by all the building work, and every night they roared in anger till the castle foundations crumbled.

'Now they were free, the dragons woke up and rose into the air, where they started fighting again. The white dragon was powerful, but the heart of the red dragon was stronger. It fought harder and longer until, at last, it overpowered the white dragon and killed it, once and for all.

'Merlin told King Vortigern that the red dragon stood for the Ancient Britons, who are now the Welsh, and the white dragon was the invading Saxons. King Vortigern built his castle somewhere else and Merlin got to live here at Dinas Emrys. That's what Dinas Emrys means – Emrys' or Merlin's city or fortress. They say he buried his gold here and that one day a golden-haired boy will come to claim the treasure!'

Harri's mum smiled and ran her hand through Harri's golden curls. 'And I suppose you think that you're the boy who's going to find the treasure, do you?'

'Well … you never know.' Harri looked hopeful. 'We might just sort of … come across it!'

'Your dad had golden hair, just like you,' his mum said, wistfully.

'And just like Merlin, I'm a fatherless child,' Harri sighed.

His mother stood up quickly. 'Come on, time to go. You're back to school tomorrow and I haven't ironed your uniform yet.'

* * *

 Down in the valley below, an old lady in a long green velvet cloak was searching for mushrooms and toadstools.

Her cloak was the colour of the moss that covered the rocks and fallen trees. Anyone looking would hardly notice her. She was almost invisible.

She saw the van parked in the lay-by and smiled as she read the name on the side.

A robin stood defiantly on a rock – his own tiny Dinas Emrys – and chirruped his fierce call. The old lady winked at him. 'Emrys has returned,' she said.

Chapter Five

 Harri woke with a start. Dylan was growling and pawing at the airing-cupboard door.

It was cold in the mornings now, so Harri put his dressing gown on and went to see what was the matter.

'What's up, Dyl?' Harri whispered, trying to calm the cat.

Bathed in the orange glow of the street light across the road, the landing was eerily quiet. Then Harri heard the noise. Dylan laid his ears flat against his head and growled. Something very small was scratching and tapping inside the cupboard!

Harri felt a wave of ice course through his veins. It wasn't fear exactly, more like he felt he was in the presence of something supernatural … a ghost?

Then he remembered the egg. For the first couple of days, Harri had checked the egg regularly but, as nothing seemed to be happening, he'd almost forgotten about it.

Slowly he opened the airing cupboard door. He moved the hand towel back.

The egg was moving! Cracks radiated from a tiny hole in the shell. *Something* inside the egg was making the hole and the cracks were getting bigger by the second. Harri remembered watching chicks

hatch under warm lamps when he was in year two. It was just the same.

The egg shook and quivered as the thing inside tap-tap-tapped, struggling to set itself free. Dylan growled again.

'Quiet, Dyl!' Harri hushed. He picked up the towel nest and carried it carefully to his bedroom where he laid it on the bed. Shooing Dylan out, he closed the door securely behind him.

With a final heave and a tiny crack, the egg split in two.

Harri gasped and held his breath. The alarm clock said 6:05 am. He must be still asleep and dreaming. He'd had dreams like that before, where he thought he was awake but he wasn't, he was only dreaming he was awake. He closed his eyes and wished that this was real and not a dream.

When he opened them again, nothing had changed. On his bed, in the middle of the nest he'd made from the hand towel, a perfect, tiny, bright-

red dragon stretched its minute wings, shook its head and sneezed.

It was the cutest, sweetest, most magical, most… Harri couldn't think of any words to describe how he felt at that moment or what he thought about the adorable creature that was sitting on his bed.

He slowly reached his hand across and ran his finger down the creature's minute, ribbed chest. It instinctively grabbed hold of him and wrapped its tail around his finger.

Harri could feel the little claws on his skin. They weren't sharp, they tickled if anything. He held the dragon up close to his face and gazed in wonder at the perfection of the tiny creature.

It blinked as it got used to the sight of its brand new world, stretching and writhing its body, now it was free and no longer squashed up inside an egg.

In the distance, Harri heard his mother's alarm clock. 'What?!' Harri's clock now said 7:00 am. He'd been staring at this incredible little thing for an

84

hour! Quick! What was he going to do? He couldn't let Mum see it.

On the way home from Dinas Emrys, they'd stopped off at the big clothes store on the edge of town and bought Harri new shoes. Harri grabbed the box and punched holes in the lid with a pencil. He laid the nest inside and put the … what was he going to call it?

'Tân!' The name just fell out of his mouth. 'Tân!' he whispered again, as he carefully placed the little creature in the box and closed the lid. 'The Welsh word for fire … perfect!'

He put the box under his bed, and placed his old shoes on top, just in case Tân was strong enough to open the lid and escape. He paused as he opened his bedroom door. *I hope he doesn't breathe fire!* he thought.

* * *

School was a nightmare. All he could think about was getting back home and seeing Tân again. He felt tired and muzzy from waking up early. His head felt groggy and all the other kids were making too much noise. He really didn't care what his friends had been doing over half-term.

'Blah, blah, blah...' Mr Davies was droning on, pointing to videos of his ancient Welsh and Saxon friends on the whiteboard. Harri tried asking a question, but his hand was so heavy he couldn't lift it.

'Are you all right, Harri?' Mr Davies' blurry face loomed over him. 'You look very pale.'

Mr Davies put his hand on Harri's forehead. Harri shivered.

'I'm so-o-o-o cold!' he groaned.

'My goodness, Harri.' Mr Davies sounded worried. 'You're burning up! You're running a temperature. I think you need to go home.'

* * *

If anyone had been watching, or if they had cared or noticed, they would have seen an old lady in a long green velvet cloak bustling down the street towards Merlin's Cave. They might have noticed the concerned look on her face – grey eyebrows furrowed with worry. They might have wondered at her straw basket, overflowing with dried flowers and plants.

And they might have noticed the old, leather-bound book that she clutched tightly under her arm.

But no one was looking, so nobody noticed.

* * *

Harri was confused. One minute he was sitting in Mrs Yates' office and the next he was in his bed at home. He had no idea how he got there.

It felt like he'd been dreaming for days. Dreaming about dragons. Big ones, small ones, red, white, every colour you can imagine, swirling around his head – fighting, clawing, gnashing, slashing, tearing each other to pieces. And in amongst them all, a tiny baby dragon being tossed in all directions, as a multitude of scaly, dragon wings churned the air into a turbulent whirlwind. He heard his mother call his name, over and over, and another woman's voice – an older woman's voice. He knew that voice from somewhere. The voices argued for a while, then both were close, talking quietly nearby. He was so thirsty. He drank something. Tea? What was that? He'd never tasted anything like it before. Ugh! Sleep… All he wanted to do was sleep … forever…

* * *

'There you are!' the old lady smiled. She sat beside Harri's bed and held his hand. Where was he? He

looked around the room. Everything was in its place. Game posters, wardrobe, dressing gown and backpack on the back of the door. Dylan was curled up on the windowsill. Everything seemed a little smaller, somehow.

'What happened?' Harri felt he was saying a line from a really bad movie. 'What are *you* doing here?'

'Dragon fever,' the old lady said, as if that explained everything.

'Dragon fever? What?' It all came flooding back to him. Harri scrambled to check under the bed. The shoebox had gone! 'Whooah!' His head spun around. He felt giddy and sick.

'It's all right,' the old lady soothed, helping him back into bed. 'Your dragon is safe and sound, downstairs. He was getting hungry. Have you given him a name?'

Harri dredged through his memories of the last few days. His head cleared slowly. 'Tân,' he said, with a weak smile.

'An excellent choice!' The old lady's eyes really twinkled.

'What does he eat?' Harri asked, 'I didn't know what to give him so I put some bread and ham in his box.'

'He seems to like worms best,' the old lady chuckled. 'The wrigglier the better. Your mother and I have been digging them up in the yard for the last couple of days.'

'Why? How long have I been asleep?'

'Over two days. Lucky I got to you in time. Dragon fever can be quite serious!'

* * *

 'Yes! That's the one for me!' Ryan's dad cheered, pressing the buy-now button. 'The Tornado 3000 ultra-light power fan. I can use the same lithium battery supply

to power the radio control system. This baby is going to fly like a dream.'

There was no lounging around watching daytime TV while there was a plane to be designed and built. The walls of his garage workshop were covered with plans and drawings of how he was going to build his J-20 Mighty Dragon Stealth Fighter Aircraft. Ryan's dad spent every spare moment reading about wing design and streamlining.

It was a good thing Ryan's mum earned a fortune at her IT business. Some of the model plane parts he was ordering on the internet were quite expensive. Every day the post man arrived with parcels of balsa wood and radio control equipment. He'd built planes when he was a kid, so he'd stop and chat to see how this project was coming together.

'Of course, it's not for me,' Ryan's dad explained. 'I'm doing it all for Ryan.'

* * *

The postman often had parcels for Merlin's Cave. The box he delivered had *Tony's Model Airplane Supplies* printed on the side. 'I'm sure I delivered this box a couple of days ago.' He sounded a little confused.

'That was quick.' Harri's mum signed the postman's little book, locked the shop door and put the *back in five minutes* card in the window.

'Look what I got on eBay!' she said mysteriously.

Harri and the old lady were in the lounge feeding worms to Tân. Harri's mum ripped open the box and pulled out a signed boxed-set of The *Happy Witch* and a bag full of *Happy Witch* goodies.

'That's Ryan's!' Harri said, surprised. 'Mrs Spelltravers told him not to sell it.'

'Well, he did and now it's yours. The *Happy Witch* really does look like you, Imelda,' she giggled, opening one of the books and looking at

the pictures. They were friends now – but their friendship had had a rocky start.

Well, what would you do if a crazy old lady turned up at your front door claiming your son might be in danger of catching a rare disease called Dragon Fever? You would think she was crazy, right? You'd probably slam the door in her face and tell her where to go. You might even think of calling the police and getting an anti-social order out against her … she was probably deranged!

But then, what would you do if you were at your sick son's bedside, waiting for the antibiotics that the doctor had given him to have an effect?

What would you do if you heard a strange scratching from under the bed and found a shoe-box and opened the lid to discover a tiny, baby dragon curled up in a nest made out of your best hand towel?

When the old lady had returned, Harri's mum invited her in and let her explain the whole story.

'Oh, he's adorable!' the old lady chuckled.

'After I'd given Harri the egg,' she explained, 'I got a little worried. I thought I'd better do some checking. I knew I'd read something about dragons and how they can be infectious when they are newborn. I've been out picking all the ingredients to make Harri well again ever since.'

There was something about her that Harri's mum trusted. After years of selling magical gifts and trinkets, she'd learned to recognise the real thing. She helped the old lady boil up her flowers, leaves and mushrooms into a gloopy tea and spooned it into Harri's mouth when it had cooled down.

Within an hour the fever broke and Harri began to sleep peacefully.

The two women became friends. They read about dragons in Imelda's ancient book to know what to feed it. Harri's mum squealed as she collected worms from the flower bed in the back yard.

'Eugh!' She jiggled in her seat, as Imelda fed the worms, one by one, to the tiny but ravenous beast. 'What are we going to do about it? We can't keep it. I mean … a dragon! This is the twenty-first century. There are probably laws against keeping dragons. They must be an endangered species. We might get sent to jail for keeping an illegal pet! What if the RSPCA found out we had a dragon?!'

'Look, the thing is, see…' Imelda pointed to a paragraph in her old book. 'It says here, "*He who*

fuffers ye fever from a Newborn Dragon and furvives shall be ye mafter of ye dragon for all time."'

Harri's mum pursed her lips. 'And what does that mean?'

'It means,' said Imelda, 'that Harri and this little dragon are joined together. Their destinies are entwined.'

* * *

 'Come on Ryan, everything's ready and the park will be empty. Everyone will be full of Christmas pudding and falling asleep in front of the telly.' It was time for the maiden flight of the J-20 Mighty Dragon.

The model was a masterpiece. They drove the hundred and fifty metres to the park and quickly turned the courtyard outside the Plas into a runway.

Ryan clicked the switches in the order he'd been

taught and stood back. The plane was magnificent – matt black with red stars on the wings. The Tornado 3000 ultra-light power fan came to life. The model shook and slowly began to move forward. In no time it was rocketing across the tarmac. Ryan's dad pulled back one of the levers on his remote control unit and the plane took off!

'One – two – three – four –' Ryan counted out loud. 'Five – six –'

The Tornado 3000 ultra-light power fan cut out. Ryan and his dad held their breath. The J-20 Mighty Dragon tipped its nose and in perfect silence, but with perfect grace, smashed into a tree, crumpling the nose and seriously damaging one of the wings.

'I don't believe it!' Ryan's dad was open-mouthed. 'It drained the battery in six seconds! There wasn't any juice left to steer it to a safe landing. We need more power if you are going to win the Dragon Gold!'

Ryan didn't know what to say. He knew how hard his dad had worked on the plane and how much it meant to him.

'Oh, well.' His dad shrugged his shoulders. 'Back to the drawing board.'

* * *

 'Let's take Tân for a walk!' Harri suggested. 'Everyone will be full of Christmas pudding and falling asleep in front of the telly. The park will be empty. No one will see.'

A lot had happened in the last few weeks. Harri had got better and gone back to school. In fact, he seemed fitter than ever. 'You've grown, Harri!' said Mr Davies on his first day back. 'What have they been feeding you?'

If only he knew, thought Harri, but he knew not to tell. What would people say if they knew

he'd been drinking a witch's brew for medicine?

Mum and Imelda had made it very clear that Tân should remain a secret as long as possible. There would be a lot of fuss if the TV and the papers found out he had a real dragon!

Imelda had moved in with them. She'd become a sort of honorary gran. She helped Mum look after the shop.

And … would you believe it? Those stinky, green love potion candles were a hit. Imelda couldn't make them fast enough. The shop had done brisk business for Christmas and the bank manager was happy again.

'Wait! Look, over there! It's Ryan and his dad.' Harri hid behind the rhododendrons and watched the short, sad flight of the J-20 Mighty Dragon.

Harri couldn't make out everything Ryan's dad said, but he heard him wail, 'We need more power if you are going to win the Dragon's Gold!'

'What are they up to?' Harri wondered as he watched the pair pack up and drive back home. 'That's not a dragon!'

Checking that no one was about, Harri opened his backpack and let Tân out for his first flying lesson.

Chapter Six

Imelda and his mum clapped themselves to get warm as Harri placed Tân on top of a tree stump. Harri gave Tân a push. Tân slid down the side of the stump, scrabbling frantically with his claws, and fell to the ground. Tân shook his head and gave Harri a look, as if to say, 'What was that about?'

Harri put him back and stretched Tân's wings to show him what he was meant to do.

The same thing happened, again and again. 'Maybe he's just not ready to fly,' Harri suggested. 'We could try again later in the week? We'd have to go up in the hills so no one can watch us.'

Just then, Tân stood up on his hind legs. His ears quivered and his eyes narrowed in total concentration. In one elegant move, his wings swept out and he leapt off the tree stump. Silently,

wondrously, he streaked through the air, landing on all fours, head down, ready to attack. With a flick of his head, he pulled a worm from the grass and swallowed it whole!

Harri stood open-mouthed. 'Did you see that?'

Imelda laughed. 'Obviously, the way to a dragon's heart is through its stomach.'

Harri searched the grass for more worms. He'd once seen a hawking display in the park. The people flying the hawks wore gauntlets on their hands. Imelda had given him some strong gardening gloves for Christmas so his hands wouldn't get ripped up by Tân's claws.

Harri held the worm between his finger and thumb. 'Tân! Come and get it!'

At the sound of his name, Tân looked up. He saw the worm and stood to attention on his back legs, erect and gimlet-eyed. Harri thrilled as Tân spread his wings, beat the air and flew straight to him. His claws grasped the leather of his glove and his jaws ripped the worm in half. The wriggling pink blob slid down his throat in one gulp before he burrowed into Harri's gloved hand for the other half.

It was the most amazing thing Harri had ever done. Mum and Imelda clapped and applauded as Harri took a bow.

'I thank you!' He laughed, taking a bow. 'Thank you, very much!' Harri looked Tân in the eye and whispered, 'That's the way to do it, you clever little thing, you!'

Tân's pupils grew huge, a sign that he was pleased to have made his master happy.

Chapter Seven

Tân wasn't so little anymore. He'd been eating and growing all over the Christmas holidays. He'd discovered that he liked sausages, Christmas pudding, St Gertrude's Pies and Dylan's cat food as well as nice fresh worms.

Dylan had got used to sharing his space. He and Tân could often be found curled up together on the landing windowsill, either basking in the weak, winter sunshine or luxuriating in the heat of the radiator.

Now the new term had started, the park was busy again. Harri would rush home from school and take Tân up the hillside behind the town. No one bothered to go there at that time of day. There he could let Tân stretch his wings and fly.

If you've never seen a dragon fly, you'll never know the thrill of watching how they twist and curl through the sky. They are quite unlike birds or bats. Dragons can hover and even fly backwards. Their

papery wings rustle while they flap them, but they're completely silent as they glide in for the kill.

A bond had grown between them. Harri only had to call and Tân would fly to his glove. He didn't need to bribe him with worms, although Tân was very pleased if there was a tasty reward when he got there!

Harri wasn't entirely alone on the hillside. He'd spotted Ryan and his dad testing out their plane one day.

After seeing them in the park on Christmas Day, Harri had gone home and done some Googling. He'd typed Dragon, Plane and Red Star into the search box and looked through the images that came up. There it was, halfway down the page, the J-20 Mighty Dragon – Chinese Stealth Fighter Aircraft. It looked just like the plane that Ryan's dad had made.

Tân was fighting with a pile of Christmas wrapping paper. Harri watched him and thought a while.

Would it be cheating if he flew a real dragon at the Eisteddfod? Wasn't he meant to have made his

108

flying dragon? He clicked onto the school website again and re-read the rules of the competition for the hundredth time.

There will be a bag of Dragon Gold for anyone who can make a dragon fly for more than ten seconds at the school Eisteddfod on St David's Day, the first of March next year.

That was as clear as mud. It didn't say what kind of dragon or what it had to be made out of. It didn't say how big or small or if it had to flap its wings.

But then again, it didn't say what the dragon couldn't be. It could be anything that could be called a dragon and it had to fly for more than ten seconds. That's all that the rules said.

'So that's what Ryan's dad is up to!' Harri smiled. 'It doesn't say the dragon can't be an airplane, just that it has to fly for more than ten seconds.'

Tân could fly for more than ten seconds … and he was a dragon! Why couldn't he enter Tân? No one could beat a real dragon at flying!

But wasn't he supposed to have made his dragon? Well, in a way he had. It was his drawing that had come to life. He'd made the drawing in the first place.

But what would Mr Davies say if he brought a real dragon to school? What would the other children say? What would the world say if the news got out that he had a real dragon? They might come and take Tân away from him and put him in a zoo!

Tân was climbing up the inside of the Christmas tree. The branches shook and all the decorations jingled and tinkled. Harri had given up trying to stop him. It was his favourite game at the moment.

Tân's head popped out just below the glass bird near the top of the tree. With a squeak of joy, he launched himself into the air and glided onto Harri's lap.

'You daft thing!' Harri laughed.

He scratched Tân under the chin – he loved that.
It made him close his eyes and go all dreamy. As Tân
relaxed, it was almost as if a spring was uncoiling
inside him.

'If only you were a remote-controlled model,'
Harri mused. 'Then I could...'

A huge grin spread across his face as he imagined
him and Tân winning the Dragon Gold and finally
beating Ryan and his dad. Maybe, just maybe, his
idea would work.

Chapter Eight

'Everything is in the box,' Ryan's dad explained for the absolute final time, as he dropped Ryan off at school. St David's Day had come at last. All his hard work was about to pay off and Ryan was going to win that Dragon Gold.

The box was so big, he'd strapped it to a trolley so Ryan could wheel it into school.

'Remember to plug it in. It needs to be completely fully charged.' He wasn't that worried. All his modifications meant that the J-20 Mighty Dragon could fly for a minute and still be under radio control for a gentle landing if the motor ran out of power.

'Yes, Dad,' Ryan sighed. He'd been rehearsed a thousand times. He knew what to do. He could fly the blooming J-20 in his sleep!

 Everyone was wearing a daffodil of one kind or another as they poured through the gates of the school. St David's Day was not only the national day of Wales but, as everyone knew, it was also the school Eisteddfod.

The children were nervous and excited. Everyone had some small part to play in the day's events. Some had larger parts and would be performing on their own. They'd been practising and rehearsing for weeks, just as Harri and Tân had been. This was a big day in the school's calendar.

A few of Harri's classmates had made attempts at making flying dragons. Mostly they were paper airplanes with pictures of dragons glued or drawn on the side. Most of them had been constructed quickly the night before. None of them were going to fly for ten seconds. They were already pretty beaten up from test flights.

Ben had had a great idea. His little brother,

Daniel, had been given a shiny, metallic balloon in the shape of a number 5 for his birthday. Ben had borrowed one of his brother's toy plastic dinosaurs and had tied it to the string of the balloon.

He was showing off his brilliant idea in the playground before assembly, when a stray football sailed through the air and slammed into his stomach. Winded and in pain, he let go and the balloon rose gracefully into the air. Many hands grabbed for it, but a gentle breeze caught the balloon and, within seconds the dinosaur was headed for the heavens. In a minute it was lost from sight in the stratosphere.

Ben's little brother stood on the infant's playground slide. He stared up to the sky. His bottom lip trembled as he wailed, 'My Blooon! My Dinysor!'

'Shush, Danny!' Ben soothed. 'Dinysoar just wants to go back home for a little while.' He turned to Harri and snarled. 'Kids! And I bet that was a winning design too!'

Harri tapped his cardboard box, to reassure himself it was still there. Tough luck for Ben but at least it was one less dragon to worry about.

Harri put his box safely on the cupboard top at the back of the classroom. He'd painted the box to look like a sort of dragon cage. It had flames swirling all over it and warning stickers too.

Keep out! Danger!
Warning – Dragons Bite!

Tân was brilliant in the box. As soon as the lights went out, he'd go to sleep for hours, until he was

brought out into the light again, when he would wake up and be almost instantly ready to play.

Ryan wheeled his box near a power socket and plugged it in. It was black with a large red star and the letters J-20 painted on the top in army style stencil lettering. The box was plastered with stickers that said *Top Secret* and warned of *Radioactivity* and *Biohazards*. Neither boy was going to show what was inside their boxes until it was time for the competition.

Harri had hardly been able to eat breakfast he'd been so excited. His tummy was rumbling from lack of food and from the butterflies he felt whenever he thought of flying Tân in public for the very first time.

'What have we got here then, boys?' Mr Davies asked as he inspected their boxes. A huge leek stuck out of the breast pocket of his jacket. You could rely on Mr Davies to make big gestures.

'You'll have to wait and see, sir,' Harri said, seriously.

116

'Oh, top secret, is it?' he asked in a conspiratorial tone. 'We won't be able to see if your dragons can fly until this afternoon, I'm afraid. We've a packed schedule this morning.'

He'd been winding them up for weeks, asking how their plans were going, making jokes about dragons and flying, asking them what they were going to do with the Dragon Gold if they won.

The boys were strangely secretive. He'd not got any information out of them at all.

* * *

The morning dragged. The whole school sat in the hall while representatives of each class came forward and showed what they had made for the Eisteddfod. Some had made clothes, others paintings and drawings, others had made models out of toilet rolls and plastic cola bottles.

Then there was the recitation competition. It

went on for hours, with poems in Welsh and English.

After break came the singing. Each class had its own choir and a song they had learned and then some children came to the front and sang on their own, while Mrs Harding played the piano for them. Megan sang something from a Disney film. Harri never knew she could sing like that. She was really good.

Then came the musicians. There weren't that many. They played violins, clarinets and recorders. Some played in duets with Mrs Harding. Rhys Evans played a pop song on his guitar. The audience jigged about and waved their hands in the air like they were at a pop concert!

Then there were silver cups and book tokens for prizes and sweets for the runners up. And then it was dinner time. The dinner ladies swept into the hall, noisily setting up the tables and chairs. They rolled up the shutters to the kitchen and in no time

the hall was full of noisy children, discussing each other's performances.

There were sausages for lunch. Harri slipped one into his pocket and looked around. Sausages were one of Tân's favourite foods.

'Aren't you going to eat those?' he asked Megan, pointing to the neat pile of sausage ends on her plate.

'I don't like the ends,' she said, making a sick face. 'Why, do you want them?'

Harri wiped the baked bean sauce off them and put them in his pocket too.

He was supposed to go outside after lunch. Mr Davies was eating a sandwich and marking some exercise books in the classroom.

'Can I just check my dragon is okay, sir?' Harry asked.

'Does it need feeding, then?' Mr Davies joked.

'Err … something like that, sir.' Harry turned his back to Mr Davies so he couldn't see what he was doing.

'Are those sausages?' Mr Davies asked. Harri froze. He hadn't been careful enough.

'Err … no, sir.' Harri scrambled for an explanation. 'Err … they're special fuel cells.'

'Oh.' Mr Davies carried on marking. 'They looked like sausages to me. Now off outside when you're finished.'

'Yes, sir, Mr Davies.' Harri breathed a sigh of relief. He'd passed that test!

* * *

'I wonder how they're getting on,' Imelda said, cutting a slice of bread for Harri's mum. 'Harri and Tân, that is.'

'I'm not sure we should have let him take Tân to school.' Harri's mum looked worried. She dipped the bread into her carrot soup. 'I don't know what will happen if anyone finds out Tân is real.'

'But the Eisteddfod is the reason Tân exists. It would be pointless for Harri not to take him. This is his big chance to beat Ryan's dad.'

Harri's mum blew on her soup. 'I suppose so,' she sighed.

* * *

Ryan's dad waited for his man-sized, chunky vegetable soup to warm up.

'Popty Ping!' he sang, as the microwave rang its little bell. He poured the soup into a bowl and stared at it for a while. He wasn't really very hungry. All he could think about was how Ryan was going to handle the J-20 Mighty Dragon and if they were going to win the Dragon Gold.

'Come on, son,' he kept muttering to himself. 'Do the business!' It was out of his hands. He felt useless.

There was nothing he could do but wait until school was over.

* * *

 It was one of those really dark, grey afternoons that you get in February and March. Mr Davies led his class out into the playground. They all wore coats and scarves. It was cold. Mr Davies looked up to the skies.

'I wouldn't be surprised if it snowed later,' he mused.

Harri and Ryan set their boxes up by the basketball hoop. The paper airplanes managed no more than five seconds in the air. Harri and Ryan were the only real contenders.

'Give them some space,' Mr Davies ordered. 'Come along, everyone go and stand against the wall. Now, who's going first? Harri … heads or tails?'

'Heads!' Harri called as Mr Davies tossed a coin into the air.

The coin spun as it landed on the ground. 'Tails! Your choice, Ryan. Do you want to go first or last?'

Ryan screwed up his eyes as he tried to judge what Harri had in his box. It would be best if he knew what he was up against.

'Harri can go first, sir.' He smiled insincerely at Harri.

Harri hoped it wasn't a bad sign that he'd lost. He opened his box and pulled out the remote control and switched it on. There was nothing inside it but a battery and a light that he'd torn out of a broken torch. The bulb was only there to make it look as if he'd switched on some complicated electronics inside.

Harri extended the aerial. He'd pulled that off an old, broken radio, and had stuck it on the side with the glue gun his mum used for packing mail orders. Ryan looked impressed. He was going to be the hardest one to fool.

123

For the past few weeks, Harri and Tân had been practising their deception. While Tân flew about in the air, Harri would wave his fake radio-control unit about as if he was making Tân fly, following Tân's movements to make it look like he was in charge.

He'd trained Tân to return to the box by giving him a nice juicy worm as his reward for doing it right.

'Are you ready, Harri?' Mr Davies called across the playground.

'Yes, sir!' Harry answered.

Mr Davies held up his stopwatch. 'I'll start counting the moment your dragon starts flying.' He winked at the other children. 'I can't wait to see this. It's powered by sausages, you know?!'

'Sausages!' The children laughed – and while everyone was distracted, Harri gave Tân the command to leave the box.

'Dragon up!'

With a flutter of wings, and a tiny mew of excitement, Tân rose gently into the air.

124

A murmur of awe and amazement swept across the tiny crowd. Harri heard a tapping and realised that all the other pupils were watching from their classroom windows.

'Wow, sir,' Ben sighed. 'It looks just like a little Welsh Dragon, it … it looks so real. It's amazing!'

Harri didn't want anyone to think Tân was real. All Tân had to do was fly for ten seconds. And that's all he did.

'Seven … Eight … Nine … Ten!' Mr Davies called. 'Well done, Harri!'

'And … dragon down.' Harri slowly lowered the aerial of his control unit until it was pointing at the box. Tân knew the signal. Gently, with a scaly, papery fluttering, he descended right into the dark interior. Harry reached into his pocket for the last bit of Megan's sausage-end as a treat. Then he closed the box and made sure it was shut tight.

He'd done it. Or rather Tân had done it. He'd behaved himself perfectly!

'That was magnificent, Harri!' Mr Davies cheered. 'A real commendation for the power of sausages! And did you make that all by yourself?'

Harri raised an eyebrow and appeared to nod. He wasn't actually claiming that he'd made Tân with his own hands, but then again, he wasn't saying that he hadn't.

Mr Davies shook his head in amazement. 'Well, Harri, that was a fantastic display. Now let's see what you can do, Ryan.'

The class cooed as Ryan opened his box and put the pieces of his plane together.

'So what sort of a dragon is that?' Mr Davies asked suspiciously.

'It's a Chinese dragon,' Ryan explained. 'It's a model of the J-20 Mighty Dragon Stealth Fighter.'

'Oh, very good!' said Mr Davies. 'Yes, I suppose that fits within the rules just fine. Did your dad help you with it?'

'A little,' said Ryan, pulling a twisted smile.

Mr Davies held out his stopwatch. 'Ready when you are, Ryan.'

Ryan switched his switches and went through his pre-flight checks. The Tornado 3000 ultra-light power fan roared into action. The plane juddered on the playground tarmac and began to roll.

The class ooh-ed as it picked up speed and then ah-ed as it lifted off the ground and woah-ed as Ryan managed to steer the plane away before it crashed into the nursery Portakabins.

He wasn't as good a pilot as his dad, who had given him strict instructions.

'Don't try to be clever. All you have to do is keep it up in the air for ten seconds. Don't do barrel rolls or take it up too steeply and stall it in mid-air. Just let it fly, nice and gently, for ten seconds.' He'd said it over and over again.

Now that the moment had arrived, Ryan felt a real temptation to show off, to dive-bomb the little crowd and give them a scare. But he knew what his

dad would say if he lost the competition. Ryan was as good as gold. He did exactly as he'd been instructed and made the plane fly around in circles.

'Seven … Eight … Nine … Ten!' Mr Davies called. 'Well done, Ryan!'

Ryan brought the J-20 into a bumpy landing and ran over to recover the craft before anyone else could touch it. It was so light and fragile, it could easily get broken.

There was an eruption of banging and tapping of windows and muffled cheering as the whole school showed their appreciation from inside.

* * *

 'Well,' said Mr Davies, back in the classroom, 'We seem to have joint winners. Two dragons flew for over ten seconds so they will have to share the Dragon Gold!'

It was just as Ryan and Harri had suspected. With a flourish worthy of a magician Mr Davies pulled a bag of chocolate money from his top drawer. The class groaned. They'd been hoping for something more special.

Secretly, so had Ryan and Harri, but they knew Mr Davies and his little jokes by now. They weren't surprised.

'So, are you going to share the prize? You can swap

around, so one of you has it one week and the other the next!' Mr Davies thought this idea was hilarious.

'I don't know,' said Ryan. It was a bit of an anti-climax. He wasn't sure what his dad would think. He'd never lost before.

Harri was disappointed too. Coming first equal wasn't actually winning, was it? He'd really wanted to win.

* * *

 Ryan's dad waited in the car. 'Act cool,' he told himself over and over. He didn't want anyone thinking that he was bothered who won!

Tiny snowflakes were falling from the sky. The latest weather forecast had threatened a real covering. It looked like school might be closed tomorrow. Good thing he had four-wheel drive on the Range Rover.

He spotted Ryan and Harri walking across the playground towards him.

'Well?' he asked, expectantly.

Ryan's shoulders dropped. He looked at Harri, pulled a face and said, 'Harri and I came equal first.'

The two boys gazed into his eyes, wondering how he'd react.

'Well … that's … w-w-wonderful,' he stammered, regaining his composure. 'So who gets the prize?' *The prize is the most important thing*, he thought to himself.

Ryan held up the bag of chocolate money. 'We share it,' he said, gloomily. 'Harri's dragon was amazing!' he told his dad. 'I don't know how he made it. It looked almost real. It flew really well.'

'Can I see it?' Ryan's dad motioned at the box.

'Err … it's kind of top secret,' Harri explained. 'You keep the Gold,' he said. 'Your plane was fantastic, you deserve it.'

Ryan's dad nodded wisely. 'We'll keep it safe while we decide what's fair.' But already his brain was

132

whirring. Somehow, he was going to win that Dragon Gold fair and square!

* * *

Ryan's dad pressed the button on the controller and the conservatory blinds rolled up, revealing a winter wonderland outside. The snow was nearly ten centimetres deep all round. It frosted the trees and made strange shapes on the birdbath and garden furniture.

'No school today!' he called up the stairs to Ryan.

He put the kettle on for a nice pot of tea and started a plan whirring around in his head.

* * *

'That's your phone bleeping,' said Harri's mum. The shop never sold anything on snow days, so she was catching up with the bills and paperwork.

133

Harri picked up the phone and read the text message. It was from Ryan.

Want to do aerial battle? Dad says the last one in the air gets the prize.

Harri felt the blood pump through his veins. Now *there* was a challenge! He knew he and Tân would win.

When and where? Harri texted back.

The challenge came back in an instant.

11 in the park, in front of the Plas.

Harri smiled. This was it.

C U there, he typed.

'I'm going to meet Ryan in the park, Mum,' Harri called from the back door. He was sneaking Tân out in his box, before Mum could work out what he was doing.

'Have you dressed up warm?' Mum called out.

'Yeah, and I've got my hat and gloves and wellies!' he shouted down the corridor.

Imelda poked her head round the shop door, winked and mouthed the words, 'Good luck!'

Chapter Nine

The streets were silent. Hardly anyone was about. The black Range Rover was parked outside the gates of the Plas. Tân's box was getting heavy now and it was hard-going, trudging through the snow.

Ryan's dad was sprinkling salt on the tarmac apron that surrounded the front of the Plas. It was where summer fetes were held and where people stood to watch firework displays.

They'd brought big red plastic snow scoops with them and cleared a perfect runway. The salt was acting quickly to turn whatever was left into a trickle of water.

'Perfect!' Ryan's dad brushed his hands together. He took his glove off, licked his finger and checked that the wind was still blowing in the right direction for the plane.

'Right,' he said, 'this is what I propose. The last

135

dragon in the air will be the winner.' He was desperate to see Harri's dragon. How could he have built something as good as his J-20?

That suited Harri just fine. He knew that the J-20's batteries would run out long before Tân was ready to call it a day. 'Okay,' Harri said, meekly. 'I'll go and get set up over there.'

Harri set Tân's box down by the rhododendrons. It was a bit warmer now and the snow was slowly sliding off the shiny, green leaves.

'This is it!' Harri whispered to Tân. 'Stay where you are until I give you the word.'

Tân looked up at him with bright, shining eyes. Harri was convinced the animal understood everything he said. Sometimes Tân seemed to do things before Harri had asked him to, almost as if he could read his mind.

'Ready?' Ryan's dad called out. Reluctantly, he gave Ryan the remote control. He had to keep reminding himself that this was between Ryan and Harri.

'Ready,' Harri replied. He winked at Tân and Tân winked back.

Harri pointed the remote control at the box and flicked the switch to turn the light bulb on. He had to keep up the appearance of being in charge of a model.

'Go!' Ryan's dad clapped his gloves together.

The Mighty Tornado 3000 ultra-light power fan wound itself up to full speed. It was much louder here, in the deadening silence of the snow. Once again, it began to roll down the runway, picking up speed, shaking and rattling, as its tiny wheels hit small bumps in the tarmac.

As it came past Harri, the front wheel lifted off the ground.

'Dragon up!' Harri ordered. Tân burst into life. He shot out of the box and hovered a metre off the ground while he took in the situation and got his bearings.

'Bloomin' heck!' Ryan's dad gasped. He knew

137

what it would take to build a model dragon, and he knew what it would take to build one that could do what he'd just seen.

Tân was in his element. He flew round the rhododendrons a couple of times and swooped up and over the roof of the Plas.

Ryan was barely in control of the J-20 Mighty Dragon. He had it set to fly in a gentle circle round the fountain and snow-covered rose beds. Tân hadn't flown with anything else before. This looked like fun. As he swooped down to investigate, his slipstream made the model plane wobble and stall for a moment.

Tân came back for more. This time his claw caught the delicate fabric of the plane's wing and tore a large gash in the surface.

Ryan's remote control began emitting an urgent beeping sound.

'Thirty-five seconds of power remaining,' Ryan announced.

Ryan's dad could not believe that he was being out-flown by a boy.

'Right! Give me that, Ryan. We are under attack. This means **WAR-R-R-R-R!**'

He grabbed the remote control from Ryan and pushed his son out of the way. Ryan tripped and landed on his bottom in a pile of slushy snow.

His dad flipped up a red cover on the control unit and let his thumb hover over a button that glowed red for danger.

'No, Dad!' Ryan called from the ground. **'Not the missiles!'**

Chapter Ten

Tân was having a wonderful time twirling and spinning around the plane. Whatever kind of dragon it was, it didn't look like him, but it didn't seem unfriendly either.

Until it started chasing him. The other dragon seemed to have changed its mood suddenly. It had a new master too, a bigger one.

Tân flipped and rolled, climbed and dived. The other dragon did the same. It was after him!

'Fire!' shouted the new master on the ground.

Bright lights burst into life under the wings of the black dragon. With a whoosh, the lights streaked towards him nearly knocking him out of the sky.

Hey! That's not very friendly! Tân thought. He turned and careered towards the ground. The black dragon banked and followed him into a ground-hugging pass in front of the Plas.

The beeping was louder now, and more urgent.

'Ten seconds of power left!' Ryan called out.

'Tân!' Harri shouted up to the sky.

Ryan's dad was determined not to lose. He had one last shot.

'Fire!' he yelled, pressing the red button so hard that it cracked under the pressure of his thumb.

Once again, Tân saw the bright red light as the firework rockets ignited and swooshed towards him. They shot past him, one on each side of his head. He felt the sparks on his ears. Right! That did it! This dragon was not friendly at all.

Tân stalled in mid-air, letting the black dragon whoosh past underneath him. Now he was back in a good position. The black dragon couldn't see him coming. He flew up until he was as high as the treetops. His heart was beating in time with that incessant beeping. He was angry with that dragon. It deserved to learn some manners.

Just as he adjusted his wings into a steep dive, the

beeping stopped and the whooshing of the dragon faded away. Silence reigned. *That dragon is up to something,* Tân thought. *It's either him or me!*

Tân dropped from the sky like a stone. Ryan's dad was bringing the J-20 Mighty Dragon into land on gliding power.

Harri was mesmerised. There was nothing he could do.

'**Tâ-â-â-â-n!**' he yelled into the sky.

A small wisp of smoke trailed from Tân's nostrils. He was almost upon the black dragon now. That dragon had really riled him, had set something burning inside, something fundamental, something essentially dragon-like, deep within him. He didn't know what it was, but he knew it was right. He knew it was dragon.

Tân took in a deep breath and roared!

'*Merde*!' Ryan's dad remembered his very worst French. Harri had just reduced his J-20 Mighty Dragon to a pile of ashes.

144

'Dragon down!' Harri ordered.

Tân, satisfied that the black dragon was no longer a danger, flew sweetly to his box and descended gently inside. Harri had no time for rewards. He slammed the lid shut, picked up the box and made to go.

'That was amazing, Harri!' Ryan's dad looked stunned. 'Aren't you going to let me see how you made it? Aren't you going to let me see what destroyed all my hard work?'

'No!' Harri said crossly. 'You started it.'

Slipping and sliding on the icy pavements, Harri rushed back home. His cheeks were red. He felt hot, bothered and angry, and he wasn't really sure why.

* * *

 Harri's mum's voice wafted up the stairs. 'Harri! There's someone here to see you in the shop!'

Harri lay on his bed, still fuming. Ryan's dad could have killed Tân with those rockets. What did he think he was doing? Once he realised Tân was going to win, he was like a baby throwing toys out of the pram. What a bad loser!

And Tân! Where did that fire come from? That ball of flame turned the plane to ash in a second and melted a huge hole in the snow too! He should never have agreed to meet them in the park. It was going to be really hard keeping Tân a secret from the world now.

'Harri! Ryan's here!' his mum called up the stairs.

What? Ryan had never been to the shop before. They were friends in school and he'd been to Ryan's house for birthday parties and things, but they weren't close friends.

Harri rubbed his eyes and told Tân to stay where he was.

Ryan was in the shop, awkwardly examining the stuff on the shelves. He had no idea what they

actually sold in Merlin's Cave. Most of it looked like girly, smelly stuff, but he knew some of it was supposed to be magic.

'I brought your prize.'

Harri took the Dragon Gold from Ryan's outstretched arm.

'You won fair and square,' Ryan said. 'Sorry about my dad. I don't know what came over him, he just lost it. I hate it when he gets like that. He could have killed your dragon!'

Harri winced. Did Ryan know the truth? The two boys locked eyes. Ryan was testing his reactions to see if he'd admit that Tân was real.

Ryan heaved his shoulders. 'You don't think I believe you made that dragon out of washing-up bottles, do you? You live in a magic shop. I saw it. It's too real not to be real.'

Harri looked long and hard at Ryan, trying to probe his mind, deciding whether he could trust him.

147

Ryan stood and waited. He wasn't going anywhere. The silence went on too long. Harri had to say something.

'D'you want a drink?'

Ryan nodded. 'Yeah, thanks!'

Harri's mum and Imelda raised their eyebrows as the boys squeezed past them and through the back room to the kitchen.

'Orange juice?'

'Yuh!'

The boys weren't sure how to start a conversation. They both knew what they wanted to talk about, but didn't know how to say it.

Harri dropped his shoulders and smiled. 'Do you want to see him?'

'Yeah!' Ryan's face lit up.

'Come on, then.' Harri led Ryan up the stairs to his room. He opened the door quietly so as not to disturb Tân.

Tân was fast asleep on the bed. He'd worn himself out. Lighting up his fires had taken a lot out of him.

'Oh – my – God,' Ryan whispered, 'he's real!'

Harri gently picked Tân up and put him on Ryan's lap.

Ryan could hardly breathe as he stroked Tân between the ears. Tân mewed quietly in his sleep.

'Oh my God, he's so cute!'

Harri didn't tell him the whole truth. When people don't understand magic, it's often best not to give them all the details. It was enough to let him know that he'd got him as an egg.

He told him all about Tân and his funny little ways. He explained how he'd seen Ryan and his dad on Christmas Day, that he'd known all along what he and Tân were up against in the competition.

'I'm fed up with my dad,' Ryan sighed. 'I wish he'd just live his own life. I never get to do anything for myself.'

Harri picked up the bag of Dragon Gold and offered Ryan one of the coins.

'Are you sure?' Ryan asked.

Harri smiled and nodded. 'This stupid Dragon Gold has caused enough trouble already. The sooner it gets eaten the better.'

'My dad's desperate to know how you made Tân fly. He can't work it out. He's such a bad loser.' Ryan unpeeled his coin and stuffed the chocolate into his mouth.

'You won't tell him, will you?' Harri was suddenly unsure.

Ryan laughed. 'I wouldn't tell him the truth about Tân if he pulled my fingernails out one by one. He can take a running jump!'

Tân woke with a start. He looked at Ryan and pounced back on the covers. He stood to attention, ready to defend himself. This was the little master that shot fire at him in the park.

'Does he like chocolate?' Ryan asked.

'I don't know. I've never given him any,' said Harri.

Ryan unwrapped another coin and offered it to Tân, who sniffed cautiously. Tân's tiny scales rustled as a wave seemed to flow down his snake-like body. His tiny barbed tongue flicked out and whipped the chocolate from Ryan's hand.

Tân made noises Harri had never heard before. Drooling, giggling, gurgling, happy noises. Tân rolled onto his side, his eyes glazed over and his eyelids drooped heavily. It was like a rubber band inside him, that held his bones together, had just snapped. Chocolate, it would seem, had a special effect on him!

Tân let Ryan pick him up and play with him. He liked this little master, even if his big master had tried to shoot him down. This little master had just given him something wonderful. It was definitely the most wonderful thing he'd ever eaten!

'I'd better bring some chocolate with me when I come and see you next time, Tân.' He laughed. '…I can come and see him again?' He left the question hanging in the air.

There was a moment's pause as Harri made up his mind.

'Of course!' he laughed. 'Now let me show you what else he can do!'

Do you enjoy drawing, like Harri? Why
not send your picture of Tân to us at
fireflypress@yahoo.co.uk?
We may be able to put it on our website.

Also in the Dragonfly series from *Firefly*

Dragonfly books are funny, scary,
fantastical and exciting.

Come to our website for games,
puzzles and competitions.

www.firefly.co.uk/dragonfly

Coming soon: Pete and the Five-A-Side Vampires by
Malachy Doyle, Dottie Blanket and the Hilltop by Wendy
Meddour and Arthur and Me by Sarah Todd Taylor.